Books should be returned on or before the
last date stamped below

For my mama and papa
-Y.R.

First published 2004 by Walker Books Ltd
87 Vauxhall Walk, London SE11 5HJ

2 4 6 8 10 9 7 5 3 1

© 2004 Yu Rong

The right of Yu Rong to be identified as the author and
illustrator of this work has been asserted by her in
accordance with the Copyright, Designs and Patents Act 1988

This book has been typeset in Shinn Extra Bold

Printed in China

British Library Cataloguing in Publication Data:
a catalogue record for this book is available
from the British Library

ISBN 0-7445-8194-X

www.walkerbooks.co.uk

A Lovely Day for Amelia Goose

Yu Rong

WALKER BOOKS
AND SUBSIDIARIES

LONDON · BOSTON · SYDNEY · AUCKLAND

Good morning, Amelia Goose!

Amelia Goose
stretches and yawns
and up she gets.

Amelia Goose goes to the pond.
"Good morning, bees.
Good morning, birds,"
says Amelia Goose.

Flip flop Flip flop

"Good morning, Amelia," say the bees and birds.

"Hello, Amelia," says Frog.
"Hello, Frog," says Amelia Goose.

"Come and play," says Frog.

Boing!

Boing!

Boing!

Amelia Goose and Frog bounce on the lily pads.

Boing!

Boing!

Boing!

They play
hide-and-seek
in the reeds.

"Boo!"
says
Amelia
Goose.

They sit on the log.

Splish

splash!

Bubbly

bubbly

bubbly

bubbly

bubbly

**All day Amelia Goose and Frog
jump and splash and play
in the pond ...**

until it's time for
Amelia Goose to go home.

"Goodbye, Frog,"
says Amelia Goose.
"Goodbye, Amelia," says Frog.
"It's been a lovely day,"
says Amelia Goose.

"Goodnight, bees and birds," says Amelia Goose.

Flip flop

"Goodnight, Amelia,"
say the bees and birds.

Flip flop

Goodnight, Amelia Goose!

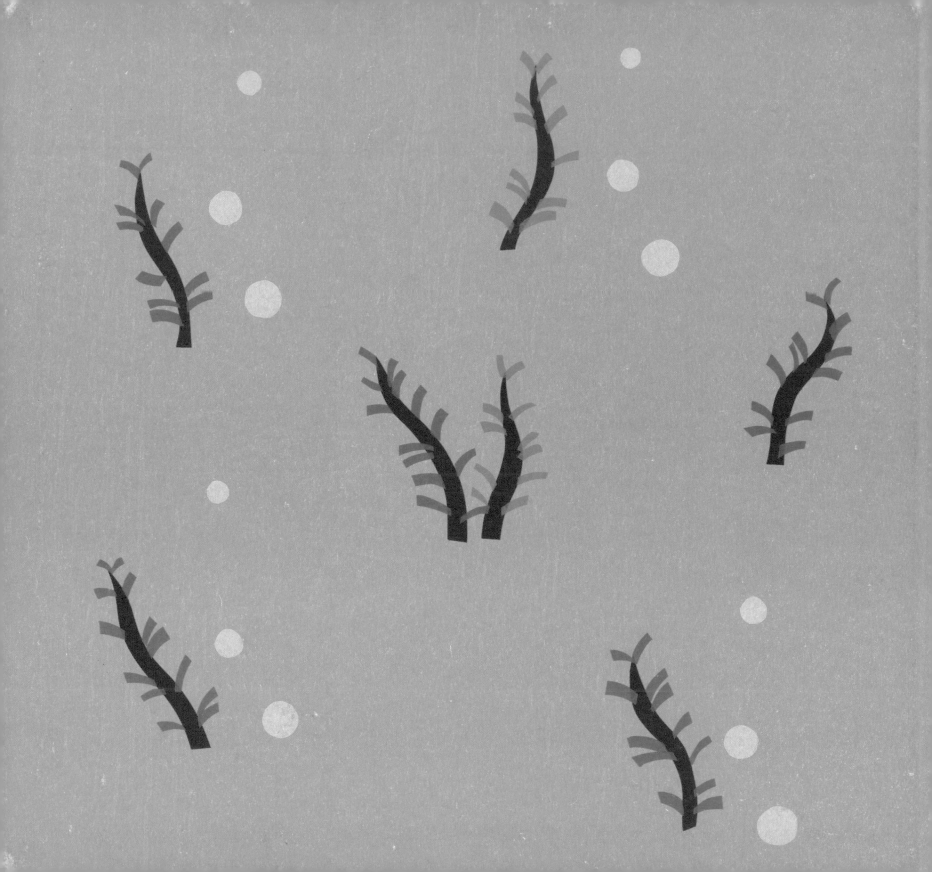